JUNE CREBBIN was a primary school teacher before taking early retirement to concentrate on her writing. She is the author of a number of books for young children including *Jumping Beany* and *Saving Oscar*, as well as several picture books.

Since childhood June has been fascinated by the story of the Norman conquest and in particular the role played by the Norman horsemen. She has visited the famous tapestry in Bayeux and walked the battlefield near Hastings on more than one occasion.

June Crebbin has two grown-up sons and two grandsons. She lives in Leicestershire.

Books by the same author

Jumping Beany

Saving Oscar

The Curse of the Skull

The Dragon Test

Emmelina and the Monster

Hal the Highwayman

Hal the Pirate

Horse Tales

No Tights for George!

Tarquin the Wonder Horse

INVASION

JUNE CREBBIN
illustrated by Tony Ross

WALKER
BOOKS

First published 2008 by Walker Books Ltd
87 Vauxhall Walk, London SE11 5HJ

2 4 6 8 10 9 7 5 3 1

Text © 2008 June Crebbin
Illustrations © 2008 Tony Ross

The right of June Crebbin and Tony Ross to be identified as author
and illustrator respectively of this work has been asserted by them in
accordance with the Copyright, Designs and Patents Act 1988

This book has been typeset in StempelSchneidler

Printed in the UK by CPI Bookmarque, Croydon, CRO 4TD

British Library Cataloguing in Publication Data:
a catalogue record for this book is available from the British Library

ISBN 978-1-4063-0502-9

www.walkerbooks.co.uk

For Averil Whitehouse
J.C.

Over nine hundred years ago, in the eleventh
century, Edward the Confessor was King
of England, ruling over the Saxon people.
He promised that, when he died, the French
Duke William of Normandy would become
king. But on his death a different man, Harold
Godwinson, was crowned King of England.
On hearing the news, early in the year 1066,
Duke William was furious. He decided that he
and his Norman soldiers would invade England,
fight King Harold and claim the crown that
he believed was rightfully his...

"My lord!"

Duke William looked up as a messenger galloped headlong into his hunting party. Rollo, his page, was holding William's horse, Firebrand. The messenger flung himself to the ground and knelt before the duke.

"My lord, I bring you news! The Saxon Earl Harold has been crowned King of England."

William went pale with anger. He paced up and down, lacing and unlacing his cloak. Like all the pages in the Norman court, Rollo knew that the English crown had been promised to William.

The duke called a meeting of his loyal noblemen.

"We will build boats to sail across the Channel!" he cried. "I will claim the crown that is mine by right. You will have lands and wealth beyond your dreams."

All that spring and summer, thousands of trees were cut down and boats were built. Boats like the Vikings had used with high, curved prows and sternposts, decorated with dragons' heads and dragons' tails: boats that were strong enough to carry horses.

By the autumn, the boats were ready, pulled up onto the mud flats of a wide river to be loaded. Along each bank were the tents of the Norman encampment. Knights, squires and pages hurried about. War horses stamped the ground. Soon the Norman army would sail to the open sea and head for England.

That is, thought Rollo, watching from the hillside, if they get everything on board in time – the soldiers with their shields, swords and spears; the barrels of wine; the servants and cooks with all their pots and pans; as well as the horses – before the wind changes.

At last he saw Firebrand, glowing like burnished copper in the sunshine. Rollo ran down the hill to be at his side. He knew the great horse would be nervous, and though Rollo

was only a page and not meant to spend much time in the stables, he practically lived there.

Planks had been laid across the soft ground to make the loading of equipment easier. But the first horses to be led forward shied away. Panic-stricken, they floundered in the mud.

"Blindfold them!" someone shouted.

But that only made the horses more nervous.

Two pulled loose, plunging and rearing through the crowd.

"Take Firebrand on first," whispered Rollo to Luc, the squire who was leading him. "If he goes on, the others will follow."

Luc grinned. He knew Rollo well. "Oh yes," he said. "You think? Well, you can help!" He swung Rollo up onto the fiery chestnut's back. "Dig your heels in!"

Rollo grasped hold of the horse's mane and urged him forwards. Firebrand hesitated, then set off at speed, as though to get across the unsure ground as quickly as possible. On reaching the boat, he jumped straight in, tipping Rollo onto the boards beside him.

Guffaws of laughter broke out as Rollo picked himself up. Stephen, the ship's boy, helped brush him down.

"It's not funny," said Rollo.

"Oh, it is!" said Stephen. "But you've done the trick."

One by one, all the horses followed, some arriving in a rush like Firebrand, some skittering along the planks in fits and starts. Once tied up in the boat, they calmed down a little as they discovered the nets full of hay that had been hung along each side.

"There's not much space," said Rollo.

"Boats aren't meant for horses," said Stephen.

"These are," Rollo retorted. "Duke William

wouldn't fight without his horses."

Within an hour, at high tide, the boats were cast off and drifted down the river to the sea.

"It's a fair wind!" shouted Rollo as he watched the sail fill.

"If it lasts," called Stephen, as he climbed to his post as look-out on the masthead. "Wind can change as quickly as a drunken man's temper!"

Rollo laughed. He set about his duties with a will: grooming the horses, keeping them calm, clearing dung and laying fresh straw where it was needed. At last, after weeks of waiting, they were finally setting sail for England. And nothing to it, he thought. All that scare-mongering by the seamen about ships tossing on the waves and seasickness. Just a gentle roll.

But when they left the shelter of the headland and reached the open sea, the boat began dipping and rising in an alarming manner. Rollo felt his stomach heave.

Stephen came down from the masthead to report to the captain.

"Duke William's boat is ahead," he said.
"The rest of the fleet is following. All's well."

Hardly had he spoken when the sky
darkened. Great drops of rain fell.

"The wind's changed!" shouted the
helmsman. "I can't hold the course."

The boat plunged wildly as the wind
strengthened. The troughs between the waves
grew deeper. Each time the boat dipped,

Rollo felt as though it would never rise again. When it did, it was only to be followed by another sickening drop.

Horses panicked, pulling back, trying to free themselves from the ropes that held them. Lightning split the sky. A horse reared up.

"Look out!" cried Rollo, as Stephen tried to make his way to the front of the boat. The horse twisted sideways and came down heavily, catching Stephen's foot beneath its hoof. Rollo pulled him clear as soon as the horse shifted.

They crouched in the bows to examine the damage. Stephen's foot was swelling. It had already doubled in size.

They heard the captain shouting to Stephen for a report.

"Can you stand?" asked Rollo.

Stephen tried. His face twisted with pain.

The captain yelled again, then caught sight of the two boys huddled together.

"Get up there!" he shouted to Stephen.

"He can't," Rollo said, standing up. His head swam. His stomach lurched. He had never felt so ill. "He's hurt."

"Then you go!" roared the captain. "You're small enough."

Rollo looked up at the masthead, rocking wildly in the wind.

"No!" cried Stephen. "The wind's too strong. You'll be blown off."

"Get a move on!" bellowed the captain. "I need to know where we are."

Rollo started to climb. He'd scaled many a tree on land and towards the top it was always shakier than below. But he'd never attempted such a thing in a wind like this and with no cross-branches to help him on his way.

Grimly he clung to the mast, wrapping his legs tightly round the pole. The wind whipped his cheeks and stung his eyes. Rain soaked through his clothes to his skin. At last, slowly, achingly, he reached the top. Rollo shook his head, trying to clear the water from his eyes, trying to see.

But what was he looking for?

Land. There was a stretch of land. Surely that wasn't right. Surely they couldn't have arrived in England so soon. Everywhere boats were being tossed like sticks in the waves. And men were in the sea, some drifting silently by, others shouting and screaming for help.

Sick to his stomach, Rollo climbed down, trying not to slide on the rain-sodden mast.

He reported to the captain.

"It's not England, you fool!" shouted the captain. "It's the coast of France. We've been blown back to our own country."

There was nothing for it but to put in to the nearest port.

Rollo was grateful to have his feet on dry land again. So many lives had been lost in the storm. The barons grumbled among themselves. "It's too dangerous," they said. "Not all the wealth and lands we have been promised is worth such a voyage as this."

But Duke William moved among them, reassuring them, urging them on, giving out generous rations. Rollo was kept busy carrying dishes of food and jugs of wine. But he escaped whenever he could to help with the horses.

"Keep your eye on the weathervane," said Luc, as they rode past the church to exercise the horses.

"Why?" asked Rollo.

"When the wind blows from the south again, then we shall try once more to set sail."

And on the fourteenth day, the weathervane swung right round. The wind had changed. It was blowing from the south.

At once, William gave his orders.

Again the fleet assembled. Again Rollo found himself on board with Firebrand and fifteen other horses. Stephen, though limping, was there too. Knights, squires and pages scrambled onto the boats, shouting to each other, all anxious to set sail.

But nothing happened.

All afternoon, the fleet waited.

The horses shifted and fidgeted.

"Why can't we go?" groaned Rollo. "The wind is right. The tide is right. What are we waiting for?"

"We're further along the coast than we were before," said Luc. "The crossing is shorter from here. We don't want to arrive in the dark."

"Why not?" demanded Rollo. "We could creep in and take the Saxons by surprise."

"We need to see where we're going," Luc replied. "We need a harbour or at least a beach."

As darkness fell, Rollo watched for the signal. At last it came. The lantern at the masthead of Duke William's boat was lit.

Quietly, without fuss, the Norman fleet crossed the Channel. As day dawned, land was sighted. The English coast!

Rollo quickly helped put on the horses' saddles and bridles. He strained his eyes as they drew closer to shore. There was not a soul to be seen.

Luc laughed. "What did you expect?" he said. "A welcoming party?"

"A battle," Rollo retorted.

"Oh, there'll be a battle," said Luc, "when we're good and ready."

One by one, the dragon ships sailed into a sheltered bay and landed on the beach. Men and horses leapt out, Duke William at their head, Rollo close behind with Firebrand.

Suddenly, William stumbled and fell.

Rollo gasped. He knew it was an evil omen. Such a fall could only mean bad luck to follow.

Quickly, he ran forward with Firebrand, and leaning down as though to give the reins to the duke, whispered urgently to him.

Duke William rose, and turning round, cried, "See. By God's splendour, I have seized England in both my hands!"

Cheering broke out. William leapt onto his horse. Knights followed suit. Luc swung Rollo up in front of him.

The Norman army galloped into England.

BATTLE!

Duke William set up camp in the nearest town.
Daily he ordered soldiers to spy out the land.
A week went by. Then at last came the news
that King Harold's army had been sighted.
William ordered a march at dawn.

"So we're going to fight at last," said Rollo.
His stomach churned. He knew that terrible
things would happen but this would be his first
experience of battle. "I can't wait!" he said.

Luc laughed. "*You* won't be going anywhere
near the battlefield!" he said.

We'll see about that, thought Rollo. He was helping Luc settle the horses for the night in one of the farms they had seized. For the past two weeks, the Normans had ravaged the countryside, taking what they wanted in the way of food and shelter. Every time they'd approached a farm, Rollo had dreaded the slaughter he knew would take place. He'd sighed with relief if it turned out to be empty. Most of the farmers and villagers had disappeared into the forests. Rollo didn't blame them. He wouldn't have hung about waiting to be killed.

"Better get some sleep," said Luc. "We start at sunrise."

Rollo lay down on his makeshift straw bed. He hadn't come all this way for nothing, he thought. He knew the battle would be fierce. He knew he wasn't old enough to fight. But he wanted to be there. He wanted to pull his weight, to help in some way.

He rose silently from his bed and crept outside. Noisy groups of men were sitting round fires drinking and talking. Rollo moved nearer. They were telling stories of past battles, laughing and boasting. One of them was showing off his scars.

Rollo crouched beneath one of the enormous farm carts that was already laden with weapons and armour. He tried to think. The pages would be left well back from the battlefield with the cooks and servants and all the non-fighting men. If he stayed with them there'd be no chance to take part.

One of the men William had sent to spy out the countryside joined a group near Rollo's hiding place.

"What news?" asked a knight. "How far do we ride to the battlefield?"

"A fair distance," replied the man, "and only one road to take us there. King Harold is camped high on a ridge. Below him slopes a field. On every side are marshes and bogs."

The men muttered among themselves. They knew the English marshland was dangerous and strictly to be avoided.

"Is the field large enough for all our troops?" asked another knight.

The soldier nodded. "Apart from a bit of scrubland, some bushes, a few trees. Nothing to hinder us," he replied.

"Except," said the knight, "that we shall be fighting uphill."

Rollo crept away. He'd had an idea.

*   *   *

Early the following day, in the chill morning air with an autumn mist lying ghost-like on the fields, the great cavalcade set off. Thousands of horses, men and heavily loaded carts clattered along the road.

Rollo, near the front, glanced behind him. The line was so long he couldn't see the end of it.

At the head of his army Duke William rode Firebrand. The great horse stepped out smartly, his chestnut coat gleaming. Rollo had groomed him to perfection.

As they neared the hill where Harold and
his army waited, the signal was given to halt.
Knights, barons and noblemen dismounted to
put on their armour. Rollo helped to hold the
horses. It was no easy task. They sensed the
tension in the air and were restless, stamping the
ground, swinging their hindquarters, champing
at the bit. They were impatient to be off.

At last the noblemen began to remount and Rollo saw his chance.

No one noticed as, quietly, he slipped away into a thicket of trees at the side of the road.

By the time the line was ready to move on, Rollo was ahead, hidden in some bushes at the very edge of the open ground. This is where the battle will be fought, he thought.

Cautiously, he peered out.

At the top of a hill, stretching along the ridge, the Saxon army was ready. Side by side they stood, their shields overlapping. How could anyone break through a wall of shields? thought Rollo. A shiver of anticipation and fear ran through his body.

Now the Norman army was taking up its position at the bottom of the slope. First came the archers, mostly armed with short bows, some with crossbows. Next came the  foot soldiers carrying swords and pikes. Behind them rode the knights, armed with swords and spears. Above them flew pennants and banners.

Rollo felt his heart fill with pride. He was proud to be Norman; proud to be a page in Duke William's court; and prouder still to be fighting for what was rightfully theirs.

Rollo withdrew and turned his attention to climbing the tallest tree in the thicket. As he did so, he heard the clanging of a thousand Saxon shields, beaten as one in a terrifying rhythm.

As he neared the top of the tree, Rollo
secured a firm foothold where the trunk forked.
Carefully, he leaned out and found that both
armies were in his sight.

The battlefield fell quiet.

Out from the ranks of the Norman troops rode
a minstrel. On he came, throwing his sword in
the air and catching it; twirling it above his head
and singing, the notes sweet and clear.

Rollo caught his breath as
the minstrel reached the middle of the
field and stopped. The singing ceased. Then,
gathering his horse beneath him, the minstrel
galloped straight as an arrow across the field;
up, up towards the Saxons. Wielding his sword,
he charged into their midst.

As he fell, the Norman archers advanced.

To the deafening blare of trumpets and horns and renewed banging of swords on shields, they loosed their first volley of arrows.

Rollo held his breath as volley after volley was fired at the Saxon line.

But the shield wall held firm. Arrows simply bounced off it. The men behind were unharmed.

William ordered his foot soldiers to scale the hill. But the slope was steep. Time after time the Norman troops struggled up to the ridge only to be driven back by a barrage

of spears, javelins, axes and stones.

Where are the horses? thought Rollo. Why didn't Duke William send in the war horses?

At last he saw the mounted knights stream into battle. Rollo scanned the field for a glimpse of Firebrand. There he was in the front lines. Trumpets sounded. Banners flew. Shouting the Norman war cry *"Dex aie*, God's help"*, Duke William and his cavalry charged up the hill.

Now the Saxons will fall, thought Rollo.

But the horses jibbed at the shield wall, trying to rear away from it, the press of horses behind them barring the way. Saxon warriors leapt forward to attack.

Rollo watched in horror as they swung their deadly two-handed axes. Horses and men were chopped down alike. Screams filled the air.

The Norman knights who were still mounted wheeled their horses round and fled. But hundreds fell into ditches and streams at the bottom of the valley.

Shouting fierce war cries, a group of Saxons broke ranks and rushed down the hill to attack the knights where they floundered in the mud.

Rollo couldn't watch. In the centre of the field, Norman horsemen were trying to fight off other Saxon pursuers, their horses plunging and rearing in panic.

A cry went up that Duke William was dead.

But Rollo could see Firebrand. He could see that the duke was still mounted.

"He lives!" shouted Rollo. "The duke lives!"
But no one heard a single voice from the edge
of the battlefield. The Normans were turning
their horses round, attempting to flee down the
hill. If their leader was dead their one thought
was to escape the terrifying axe men.

Rollo scrambled down the tree, swung
himself up onto a riderless horse and galloped
towards Firebrand.

"My lord!" he gasped to the duke. "Lift up
your helmet so that your knights can see your
face. They think you are dead!"

At once William did as Rollo suggested.
"I live!" he cried. Shouting and threatening
with his sword he rallied his troops, forcing
those in flight to turn around.

Suddenly Rollo realized he was in the thick of the battle. On every side, soldiers were slashing and slicing. Stabbing and hacking.

He wheeled his horse around. But as he did so, he felt a searing pain in his leg, and fell, hitting the ground head first.

*　　*　　*

When Rollo opened his eyes, he was lying in a hollow. Above him stars like tiny sparks lit the darkening sky.

He heard voices. Muffled talking, cries of pain, moaning. Dark shapes moved back and forth.

Rollo lay still. He'd heard enough stories about warfare to know that pretending to be dead would be his best chance of survival.

After a while, as no one had come near him, he lifted his head, but it was as though a thousand drums were beating inside his skull. He lay down again quickly.

"You're alive then!" said a voice. Luc bent over him. "Mad fool that you are!"

Rollo managed to raise himself up a little.
"Is the battle over?" he asked.

Luc nodded towards a solitary figure on
the hilltop, moving among countless bodies.

"There's the King of England!" he said.

"But is it Harold or William?" whispered
Rollo.

Luc laughed. "William, of course!" he said.
"After your appearance on the battlefield we
went from strength to strength."

Rollo listened intently as Luc told him how Duke William had ordered his archers to fire high into the air over the Saxon shield wall so that the arrows rained downwards, killing the men behind; how the duke had sent in his horsemen to attack and then *pretend* to turn and flee; and how the Saxons had broken ranks and chased the Normans down the slope.

"But, at the bottom of the hill," finished Luc, "our troops turned, taking the Saxons completely by surprise, and attacked them! From that moment, the Saxons were beaten."

"And Harold?" asked Rollo.

"Killed by an arrow in the eye, they say," said Luc. "Not long after I'd seen you fall and dragged you to safety."

Despite himself, Rollo felt his eyes closing. Luc had assured him the gash in his leg was not deep but it throbbed insistently as did the pain in his head. But there was one more thing he needed to know.

"Firebrand?" he said. "Is he all right?"

Luc shook his head. "I'm sorry, Rollo. Firebrand was a hero. He carried William bravely, charging again and again but, in the end, even he couldn't escape those terrible axes."

Rollo sank back. He felt as though someone had punched him, had knocked all the strength out of him.

"You need rest," said Luc. "We all do. Five days we're allowed."

"And then?" asked Rollo.

Luc stood up. "And then," he said, "we march to London!"

THE KING IS CROWNED

Rollo trudged along the road in silence.
He was cold, wet and hungry. The Norman
army had been on the move for weeks.
One day, they marched; the next, they
rested. If you could call it rest, thought Rollo.
Pages were ordered to search for food and
firewood on the rest day.

Rollo could just about bear the bleak November weather with its constant drizzly rain but the hunger pains in his stomach never went away. Pages were the last to be given food. Coarse bread and soup might come their way eventually. But not meat. That was saved for the noblemen.

Rain fell relentlessly as they marched. Rollo felt that it seeped into his very bones. He ached with tiredness. At the front of the line, William rode a black charger. Rollo thought longingly of Firebrand. Several of the barons and knights had lost their mounts. Now they rode on ponies, seized from the Saxons after the battle. They made a sorry sight.

At last the straggly line halted. It was late afternoon, gloomy and chill. The army camped in a desolate farmhouse on a hillside. Rollo helped Luc to settle the horses and ponies.

"How far to London now?" asked Rollo. He asked the same question at the end of every day's marching, and the answer was always the same. Luc didn't know.

"All I've heard is that William is biding his time," he said.

"What for?" said Rollo.

"He doesn't want to enter London until he knows it's safe," said Gilbert, the Captain of the

Guard, who was looking after his own horse.

"But he's the king!" cried Rollo. "He's William the Conqueror, King of England!"

"*We* know that," agreed Gilbert, "but until he's crowned..." He shrugged and walked away.

Rollo knew well enough that, though many of the Saxon nobles supported William, others didn't want him as their king, even though he'd won the battle. But William knew he was the rightful king. He'd had to get rid of the rebels who opposed him. So why couldn't he march into London and get himself crowned?

Rollo made sure the last pony was well rubbed down before he set about finding a bed for the night. No use trying the farmhouse or the barns. They'd be occupied by knights and noblemen. He looked outside and found a corner in a squat, stone building, open to the sky but out of the wind. From the smell of it, Rollo guessed, pigs had used it last!

He curled himself up into a ball, wrapping his arms tightly around his knees, trying to instil enough warmth into his body to be able to sleep. He thought about the coronation. He imagined himself dressed in rich, royal colours; trumpets heralding the new king;

tables laden with spiced meats, fish and fruits
– a banquet fit for a king! And his pages!

Dreaming of such wonders, Rollo slept.

The following morning, Rollo was rudely
awoken by one of the cooks prodding him
with a stick.

"Up, up, you lazy good-for-nothing!"
shouted the cook. "How can I light the
fires with no wood?"

Rollo tried to move. His limbs ached. His legs refused to straighten. But the cook carried on prodding until Rollo struggled to his feet.

On the other side of the valley was dense woodland. Plenty of firewood, thought Rollo, but so far to go. It would take a long time to get there and even longer to return, weighed down with sticks and logs. If only he had a pony to help him. Rollo groaned. No chance of that.

Perhaps, he thought, he should *borrow* a pony! No one would miss it so early in the morning. The noblemen slept until noon on their rest day. They only stirred when the smell of food hit their nostrils.

Quietly, Rollo made his way across the farmyard to where some of the ponies were tethered. He untied the first one he came to, threw saddle bags over its back, grabbed a length of rope, and leapt on.

Oh, the joyous freedom of cantering full tilt down the hill! Rollo felt as if he was flying.

At the bottom of the valley, he jumped off to drink the clear cold water of a stream, the pony doing likewise. Then, at a brisk trot, they set off up the hillside and entered the wood.

It was so dark that, at first, Rollo found it difficult to see anything clearly. But before long, the trees thinned a little. Grassy tracks emerged. Rollo worked hard at filling the saddle bags with kindling. He needed to find some good-sized logs too, and he couldn't be long.

Acorns littered the track and then he found beech nuts, masses of them. He stripped away the shells and stuffed the nuts into his mouth. This was the best meal he'd had in weeks!

Rollo walked on, forgetting about the firewood, intent only on gathering and eating.

But suddenly he was aware of something coming towards him through the trees, snorting and grunting.

A wild boar!

On it came, snuffling and chomping.

Rollo felt for the knife in his belt. He slapped the pony on its rump, sending it galloping away, as the young boar, snout to the ground, stepped into the open.

Rollo waited, his fingers closing round the hilt of his knife. He knew he had one chance and one chance only. Wild boar were known for their ferocity. If Rollo wounded it, the boar would become even more fierce. He had to go for its throat.

Rollo moved forward. At the same moment, the boar looked up, saw him and charged!

Its speed took Rollo by surprise. Before he had time to raise his knife, the boar was on him, crashing him to the ground.

Rollo lay winded. His head swam. But he sat up. He knew the boar would charge again.

He stood, his hand steady on the knife. But the boar had disappeared into the trees.

Terrified screams hit the air. With horror, Rollo realized it was attacking the pony.

Rollo ran into the trees. The pony was on its hind legs, lashing out with its forelegs, but the boar was going for its underbelly with its sharp tusks.

Rollo flung himself forward, burying his knife deep into the boar's throat.

The pony's hooves flashed above him. Then the boar slumped over, blood gushing from its body. He'd done it!

Rollo hurried to the pony. But someone was there before him – a girl – calming it, soothing it. Leading it away.

"Wait!" cried Rollo.

The girl quickened her pace, but the undergrowth was thick beneath her feet. Twice she stumbled, then she fell.

Rollo reached her and grabbed the pony's halter.

"What do you think you're doing?" he yelled. "Stealing a pony!"

The girl glared.

"Storm's mine!" she shouted, getting to her feet. "You stole him from me!"

Suddenly, Rollo realized the girl had replied in his own language. She understood French. Yet she must be Saxon. She sprang forward to seize the pony.

Rollo blocked her with his shoulder, pushing her away.

"How do you know French?" he demanded.

He had to repeat the words and his actions two or three more times before the girl stopped trying to get past him and gave in. Rollo saw then that she was just as tired, hungry and low in spirits as himself.

"Tell me," he said.

"Then you'll let me have my pony?"

Rollo didn't answer.

"My name's Mary," she told him. "I've been following you for weeks waiting for a chance to rescue Storm."

Rollo looked at the pony. Storm was a good name. He was a beautiful iron grey. If he was my pony, he thought, I wouldn't want to lose him.

Mary told him she'd been brought up in a manor house near an abbey. The Norman monks had taught her French.

She reached for the pony.

Rollo hesitated. If he managed to drag the wild boar back with him, he'd be the toast of the camp. No one would miss one small pony. Anyway, even if they did, ponies sometimes broke loose from their tethers and went wandering off.

Rollo removed the saddle bags and handed Storm over.

"Where will you go?" he asked.

"To London," said Mary. "That's where my family will be by now."

"That's where we're heading!" said Rollo. "To the coronation."

"I know," said Mary.

Rollo watched her leave, then, hoisting the still bleeding carcass of the boar across his shoulders and carrying the firewood and

saddle bags as best he could, he began his slow
descent down the hillside.

A watery sun came out. Rollo stepped
forward more briskly. At least he'd caught
a boar. Maybe this would put a smile on the
cook's face? The soldiers would feast tonight!

Christmas Day, the day of William the
Conqueror's coronation, dawned crisp and clear.

Rollo dressed quickly. It was hard to believe
he had clean clothes again and was living in a
wooden castle, which William had insisted on his
men building before he entered the city of London.

William was to be crowned in the new abbey
of Westminster. Rollo was disappointed that

he wouldn't be going inside the grand building, but Gilbert had chosen him as one of the pages to attend to the horses outside.

Crowds of people, both Norman and Saxon, had gathered to watch. Some tried to scramble up the abbey walls to peer in through the windows. Others kept surging forwards, trying to break through the line of Norman horsemen in order to see what was going on.

The horse Rollo was holding kept rearing and bucking. Rollo felt as if his arms were being pulled out of their sockets. Surely the service would be finished soon.

Suddenly, from inside the abbey, came shouting. A pause, and then more raised voices.

The Norman guards drew their swords.

"The Saxons are killing our king!" they cried, slashing out at the nearest onlookers. They seized flaming torches and set fire to the houses close by.

The crowd scattered, screaming. Horses stampeded. People were trodden underfoot.

Rollo fought to keep hold of his horse.

"They're not killing him," said a voice at his side. "They're wishing him a long life." It was Mary. "They're shouting 'Long live the king!'" she said.

Gilbert was trying to control his men.

"Tell him," urged Mary, "or we'll all be killed."

She took hold of Rollo's horse.

Rollo forced his way through the crowd to Gilbert and told him what was happening.

Gilbert hesitated. Then the huge doors of the abbey opened.

"See for yourself!" cried Rollo.

Gilbert spurred his horse forward.

Seated on a great throne in front of the altar was William, the crown upon his head, bishops and ministers at his side.

"Long live the king!" shouted the Saxons.

"*Vive le roi!*" shouted the Normans. "Long live King William!"

THE SWALLOW AND THE FIREFLY

Rollo stood at King William's side holding a silver bowl filled with water. He wished he was back in London where everything was busy and bustling. It was so quiet here in the fens. Life was as flat as the marshland stretching away into the distance all around them.

The king was having lunch. At any moment, he might finish his meal and want to wash his hands before going hunting. Rollo longed for him to do so. Once the hunting party had left, he could slip away to the stables. A new load of horses had arrived from France that very morning and he wanted to see them.

William seemed in no rush. He was too busy holding counsel with his noblemen about how to conquer the Saxon rebels who plotted to kill him and reclaim the crown.

"Breathe not a word of our plans," he warned.

"But will we succeed, my lord?" asked a knight. "The Saxons know their land. We don't. These fens are treacherous."

William hit the table with his fist. "I know that well enough!" he shouted. "Haven't I lost countless men in this mud and slime?"

"The Saxons travel through the fens like slippery eels," persisted the knight. "They hide behind reeds. They take their boats into channels we cannot even see."

William stood up. At last, thought Rollo, offering the bowl. But the king was still talking.

"We will succeed," he said, "when our new fleet of boats comes from France; when we build a road to carry our army; when we set fire to their reeds. Then we shall see their channels. Then we shall force these rebels out of their hiding places!"

The nobles cheered.

"And catch their leader Hereward!" someone shouted.

"He's the most slippery eel of all," said another. "You never know where he'll turn up next."

"Be on your guard," said William. He turned to Rollo, washed his hands and strode away.

Rollo flew to the kitchen, rinsed out the bowl and ran to the stables.

Mary was there, feeding her pony, Storm.

"I've seen the new horses," she said.

"How many are there?" demanded Rollo. He tried not to show his annoyance at Mary beating him to it. Now that her father was the court's interpreter, constantly at William's side, Mary often knew things before he did. *And* she could visit the stables any time she liked. Her only duty was to translate English into French, or French into English, like her father. She was needed mainly in the kitchens or in the living quarters with the ladies.

"Sixteen," replied Mary. "Come on, I'll show you."

Rollo followed her into the stables. Everywhere that William travelled, a castle was built, which, though made of wood, was strong enough to protect him from any Saxons who didn't want him ruling over them.

Rollo walked along the stalls, marvelling at each new inhabitant.

"Aren't they magnificent?" he said. "*Destriers.* War horses. Not your puny ponies!"

"Our ponies were good enough for you once," Mary reminded him.

Rollo ignored her. He was staring at the last horse in the row, a bright chestnut stallion. Luc was brushing his mane.

"What do you think?" he asked Rollo. "This is Firefly, Firebrand's son."

Rollo found his voice. "He's wonderful," he said. "Have you ridden him?"

Luc nodded. "He covers the ground like the wind sweeps through the sky," he said.

"I saw you," said Mary. "But he's not as fast as Hereward's mare Swallow. She's as swift as a bird!"

Luc frowned. "Hereward the Wake?"

"They call him that because they say he's always awake," said Mary. "You'd never catch him napping!"

"I know he's causing a lot of trouble," said Luc.

"That's because he won't accept William as king the way we do," said Mary. "My family has always been friendly towards the French, especially the Normans, ever since the time of the old king, Edward the Confessor."

Luc nodded approvingly.

Rollo was still staring at the stallion. He longed for a horse of his own. He'd been put on a pony almost before he could walk. He knew how to ride; how to groom; how to feed and exercise a horse. Yet he wouldn't be given one until he was a squire.

"I wish he was mine," he breathed.

Luc laughed. "If wishes were horses..." he said.

"I'll get my own one day," retorted Rollo.

Luc shook his head. "It won't be this one," he said. "He'll be taken long before you're of an age." He handed Rollo a brush. "But you can finish grooming him if you like."

Rollo brushed Firefly until his coat shone. He cleaned his tack and mucked out his stable.

"There's others to see to as well," Luc reminded him.

By late afternoon, everything was in order. The hunting party returned. Rollo helped rub down the tired, sweating horses, making them comfortable. But his mind was on Firefly.

He felt restless. He knew he should go back to the castle, help get the tables ready for dinner, play his lute to entertain the ladies. But he couldn't settle.

"I'm going out," he said.

"Don't be long," warned Luc. "You've other duties, you know."

Rollo made his way to the wooden fence that encircled the castle. He climbed the ladder up to the walkway where the guards kept watch, and looked out over the fens.

It was a desolate scene. Beneath a slate-grey sky, reed beds covering sludge and slime stretched as far as the eye could see. Only a single narrow track wound its way up to the castle.

Suddenly Rollo saw a figure in the distance, fast-approaching on horseback. Drawing nearer, the rider pulled up sharply and dismounted. It seemed as though he was attending to something on the horse's back but he was still too far away for Rollo to see clearly. Eventually, the rider remounted and rode on at a much more

leisurely pace.

At the castle gates, he jumped off and tethered his horse. He untied two saddle bags and, slinging them round his neck, strode into the castle shouting, "Pots for sale! Pots for sale!"

The cooks came out eagerly from the kitchens to greet the potter and find out what he had to offer. Rollo went to examine his horse. But the mare was nothing much to look at. She had a great chuckle-head set on a long skinny neck, a thin rangy body and drooping hindquarters.

"Race you!" cried Mary, appearing at Rollo's side on Storm. "You'll never catch me on that thing!" She sped off along the track.

Rollo looked round quickly. No one was watching. The potter would be a while yet, plying his trade.

Rollo loosed the mare's rope, leapt onto her back and dug his heels into her bony flanks. At once he felt her lift and respond. She leapt forwards. Rollo caught his breath. The wind whipped past his ears. His eyes streamed. His mount covered the ground in long flowing strides. Easily, she gained on Mary and Storm, overtook them, and galloped on. She was tireless. Who would have thought such a creature could move so quickly?

At last, Rollo drew the mare to a standstill
and turned. Mary had given up and was riding
back towards the castle. Rollo followed at a
walk to cool down. He hadn't gone very far
when he noticed a heap of broken pots at the
wayside. Rollo frowned. How strange that a
potter should have ridden at such a speed as to
break so many of his pots! It was a wonder he
had any left to sell!

The more Rollo thought about it, the more he
puzzled. A potter wouldn't own a horse like this
anyway. For all her grim appearance, she had
great quality and speed; she was as swift as a bird.

Suddenly, a terrible thought struck Rollo. Once more he dug his heels into the mare's flanks. If his fears were right, King William was in danger. Rollo sped back to the castle, jumped off his mount, tethered her and ran to the kitchens. Mary was already there.

"You're late!" she scolded. "King William is at dinner." She handed him the silver water bowl.

"But what of the potter?" gasped Rollo.

"What potter?" said Mary.

"He's in the great hall," said a cook. "He insisted on showing off his pots, though we have relieved him of most of them!"

"The king is in danger!" cried Rollo.

He rushed into the hall, trying not to spill the water as he went.

"My lord!" he cried.

William waved him to one side. The potter was before him, holding up a jug.

"You may think this is a simple earthenware jug—" began the potter.

Rollo stepped forward. "My lord," he pleaded. "I beg you to listen to what I have to say—"

"Silence!" roared the king. He turned to the potter. "So what is so special about it?" He laughed. "Does it contain jewels? Does it hold silver and gold?"

"A jewel indeed!" cried the potter and, putting his hand inside, he drew out a dagger. He leapt forward onto the platform where King William was sitting, the jug crashing to the floor, the dagger held high, aimed at the king's heart.

Rollo leapt too. He threw the water from the silver bowl straight into the potter's eyes, blinding him, if only for a moment. But it was enough.

"This man is no potter!" cried Rollo. "He is Hereward. His mare, Swallow, is tethered at the gate!"

William was quick to draw his sword but Hereward was quicker. He tipped up the table and sent the king and several of his noblemen sprawling. Then he jumped off the platform onto the table below and raced along it, scattering pots in all directions. He sprang across to another table, then another and yet a third before dropping to the floor.

Soldiers drew their swords, shouting "Seize him! Seize him!" but Hereward dodged round them as if they weren't there.

Out of the door he ran, and across the courtyard to the castle gate. In a flash, he loosed Swallow, sprang onto her back and, crying "Awake! Awake!", galloped away.

"Fools!" shouted William, as the news was brought to him that Hereward had escaped. "You had him in your grasp and you let him go!"

He stormed out of the hall.

*　　*　　*

Some time later King William sent for Rollo.

Rollo entered the royal chamber and knelt on one knee before him. But the king commanded him to rise.

"You have served me well," he said, "ever since we set sail from Normandy. I remember how you came to my aid on the beach, and then again in the heat of the battle, and today you saved my life."

Rollo moved as if to speak. He wanted to say it was an honour to serve such a king. But William held up his hand.

"You are full young to become a squire," he continued, "but that is what I wish. Do you think you can carry out the necessary duties? Will you be at my right hand when I'm hunting? Can you be at my side when I go into battle?"

Rollo hesitated.

"What?" said William. "You cannot?"

Rollo spoke up. "I would need a horse."

William roared with laughter. "Any!" he said. "Go and make your choice! There are new ones in the stables even now."

Rollo rushed straight to Fi... arms round his neck. "I'm g... he whispered, burying his fa... chestnut coat. "I can choose an...

He stood back. Firefly loo... expectantly. Rollo reached forw... his arms once more around his h...

"Together," he said, "we will serve King William all our days!"